Flip the Flamingo

by **Penny Dolan** and **David Arumi**

W
FRANKLIN WATTS
LONDON•SYDNEY

Flip was a baby flamingo.

He lived by the big lake

with his mum and dad.

Mum and Dad
had very long legs
but Flip's legs were short.

5

"Can I come into the water, too?"
said Flip.

"Not yet," said Mum.

Day by day, Flip got bigger

and his legs grew longer.

One day, Mum said,

"Come into the water, Flip."

Flip went into the water.

He stood very still,

just like Mum and Dad.

Flip looked down.

"Help!" he said.

"I have just one leg."

He did not want to fall over.

Then Flip saw Mum and Dad.

They stood on one leg, too.

"Oh, good!" said Flip.

Flip looked for his other leg.
He found it, tucked up
under his feathers.

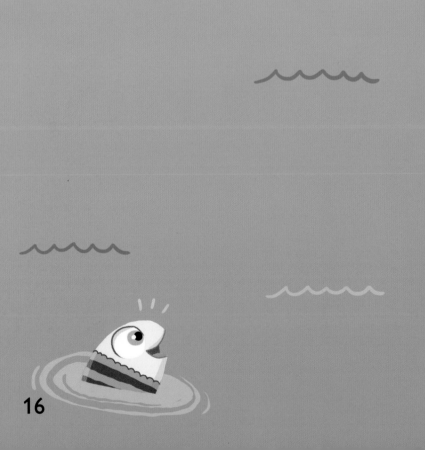

Flip put his leg into the water.

One leg! Two legs!

Just like his mum and dad.

Story trail

Start at the beginning of the story trail. Ask your child to retell the story in their own words, pointing to each picture in turn to recall the sequence of events.

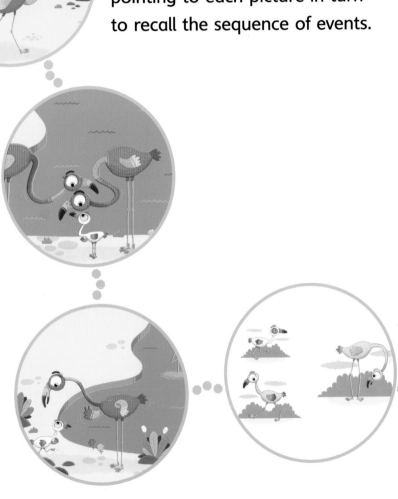

Start

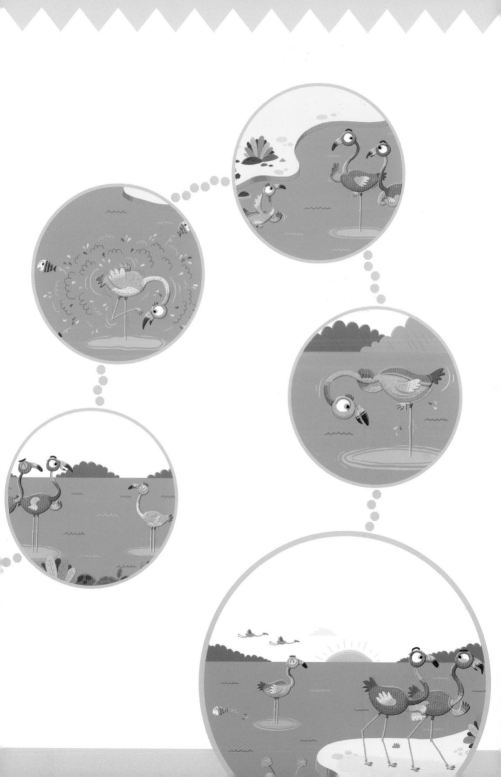

Independent Reading

This series is designed to provide an opportunity for your child to read on their own. These notes are written for you to help your child choose a book and to read it independently.

In school, your child's teacher will often be using reading books which have been banded to support the process of learning to read. Use the book band colour your child is reading in school to help you make a good choice. *Flip the Flamingo* is a good choice for children reading at Blue Band in their classroom to read independently.

The aim of independent reading is to read this book with ease, so that your child enjoys the story and relates it to their own experiences.

About the book

Flip is eager to go in the water, like his mum and dad. But he must wait until he is old enough, and learn how to use both legs!

Before reading

Help your child to learn how to make good choices by asking: "Why did you choose this book? Why do you think you will enjoy it?" Look at the cover together and ask: "What do you think the story will be about?" Support your child to think of what they already know about the story context. Read the title aloud and ask: "Which Flamingo do you think is Flip? Who else can we see with Flip?" Remind your child that they can try to sound out the letters to make a word if they get stuck.

Decide together whether your child will read the story independently or read it aloud to you. When books are short, as at Blue Band, your child may wish to do both!

During reading

If reading aloud, support your child if they hesitate or ask for help by telling the word. Remind your child of what they know and what they can do independently.

If reading to themselves, remind your child that they can come and ask for your help if stuck.

After reading

Use the story trail to encourage your child to retell the story in the right sequence, in their own words.

Support comprehension by asking your child to tell you about the story. Help your child think about the messages in the book that go beyond the story and ask: "Why did Mum stop Flip going in the water at the beginning of the story? What did Flip learn?"

Give your child a chance to respond to the story: "Did you have a favourite part? What did you learn about Flamingoes from reading this story?"

Extending learning

In the classroom, your child's teacher may be reinforcing punctuation and how it informs the way we group words in sentences. On a few of the pages, ask your child to find the speech marks that show us where someone is talking and then read it aloud, making it sound like talking. Find the question marks and exclamation marks and ask your child to practise the expression they used for questions and exclamations.

Franklin Watts
First published in Great Britain in 2017
by The Watts Publishing Group

Copyright © The Watts Publishing Group 2017

Series Editors: Jackie Hamley and Melanie Palmer
Series Advisors: Dr Sue Bodman and Glen Franklin
Series Designer: Peter Scoulding

A CIP catalogue record for this book is
available from the British Library.

ISBN 978 1 4451 5479 4 (hbk)
ISBN 978 1 4451 5480 0 (pbk)
ISBN 978 1 4451 6090 0 (library ebook)

Printed in China

Franklin Watts
An imprint of
Hachette Children's Group
Part of The Watts Publishing Group
Carmelite House
50 Victoria Embankment
London EC4Y 0DZ

An Hachette UK Company
www.hachette.co.uk

www.franklinwatts.co.uk

FSC
www.fsc.org
MIX
Paper from
responsible sources
FSC® C104740